THIS WALKER BOOK BELONGS TO:

_____

_____

_____

For Kitty and Kate
D. M. ~

For Deirdre and Lucy
~ S. H.

First published 1996 by Walker Books Ltd
87 Vauxhall Walk, London SE11 5HJ

This edition published 1997

10 9 8 7 6 5 4 3 2

Text © 1996 David Martin
Illustrations © 1996 Sue Heap

This book has been typeset in Cheltenham Book.

Printed in China

British Library Cataloguing
in Publication Data
A catalogue record for this book is available
from the British Library.

ISBN 0-7445-5236-2

LITTLE CHICKEN CHICKEN

by David Martin

illustrated by Sue Heap

WALKER BOOKS
AND SUBSIDIARIES
LONDON • BOSTON • SYDNEY • AUCKLAND

Little Chicken Chicken and Baby Chick were scratching in the garden with the other chickens.

"Look," said Little Chicken Chicken, "I found a string. I'm going to make a tightrope out of it."

"That's nice, dear," said her mother.

The other chickens looked up and laughed at Little Chicken Chicken.

"Some tightrope!" they said.

Little Chicken Chicken put her string in a box

inside the chicken coop and started doing backflips.

The next day she found
two round black stones.
"Look at these stones,"
she said. "They fell out
of a thunder cloud.
See, that's why
they're so dark."

"Oh, *really*," said the rooster. And he and the big chickens all laughed.

Then the little chickens
began to tease her.

One of them had a bent nail.
"Here's another thunder cloud,
Silly Chicken Chicken."

"And here's some wind,"
they said. And they blew
dandelion fluff at her.

That afternoon,
Little Chicken Chicken
found a sparkling glass bead.
She put it away with her
other toys and didn't tell
anyone about it.

Soon the wind picked up and ruffled the chickens' feathers. "Feels like it's going to rain," said Little Chicken Chicken's mother.

Lightning flashed and thunder shook the ground.

It began to rain hard.

The chickens ran into the coop and huddled together. Suddenly the wind blew away a piece of the roof.

"Ahhh!" screamed the little chickens, and they began to cry.

"Help!" screamed the big chickens, and they began to shake.

"Oh," said Little Chicken Chicken, "my toys are getting soaked!" She flew down to save them and then began to play.

She strung up her string, hopped on to it and balanced on one foot.

"Look," someone whispered. "Look at Little Chicken Chicken."

And as lightning lit up the coop, she did a backflip off the string ...

and a cartwheel across the floor!

The rooster applauded.
"Ladies and gentlemen," he said,
"it's Little Chicken Chicken's
Thunderstorm Circus."
"Do more. Do more,"
everyone said. "Please."

So Little Chicken Chicken
jumped back up on the string.
She held up her two black
stones and said, "My friends,
these stones are from the
heart of a thunder cloud."

And then, with a wave of
her wing, she made the
sparkling glass bead appear.
"And this is a piece of
lightning I grabbed as it
flashed across the sky."

"These things are so magical they will fly in the air before your very eyes."

And she tossed them up and began to juggle.

Everyone cheered.

Soon all the chickens were doing backflips and trying to juggle and falling off the string.

"Was that true? Did that bead really come from lightning?" Baby Chick asked her mother.

"I don't know. Ask Little Chicken Chicken."

But just then the rain stopped and everyone went outside.

"Look, I found a thunder stone," said one little chicken.

"Me too," said another. "And I found a piece of lightning."

But Little Chicken Chicken didn't hear them.

She was too busy chasing grasshoppers.

"Watch out!" she shouted.

"Leaping dino-monstersaurs!"

"Wait for us!"
the other chickens said.

And off they went,

jumping and shouting

and flapping across

the garden.

MORE WALKER PAPERBACKS
For You to Enjoy

FIVE LITTLE PIGGIES
by David Martin/Susan Meddaugh

Why did this little piggy go to market and this little piggy stay at home?
And what about the little piggy that went wee wee wee? What's his story?
These five funny tales, each inspired by a line of the
favourite rhyme, tell the whole hoggy truth!

0-7445-6346-1   £4.99

MRS GOOSE'S BABY
by Charlotte Voake

Shortlisted for the Best Book for Babies Award

There's something very strange about Mrs Goose's baby –
but her mother love is so great that she alone cannot see what it is!

"An ideal picture book for the youngest child." *The Good Book Guide*

0-7445-4791-1   £4.99

GRANDAD'S MAGIC
by Bob Graham

Grandad's magic may not be big magic, but it's large enough
to cause a stir in Alison's house one Sunday lunchtime!

"Full of neat asides and significant details… Excellent."
The Times Educational Supplement

0-7445-1471-1   £3.99

Walker Paperbacks are available from most booksellers, or by post from B.B.C.S., P.O. Box 941, Hull, North Humberside HU1 3YQ

24 hour telephone credit card line 01482 224626

To order, send: Title, author, ISBN number and price for each book ordered, your full name and address,
cheque or postal order payable to BBCS for the total amount and allow the following for postage and packing:
UK and BFPO: £1.00 for the first book, and 50p for each additional book to a maximum of £3.50.
Overseas and Eire: £2.00 for the first book, £1.00 for the second and 50p for each additional book.
Prices and availability are subject to change without notice.